GW01326079

THE DANGEROUS
WORLD OF
STUFF AND THINGS

THE DANGEROUS WORLD OF STUFF AND THINGS

by
Kevin Upton

First published in the United Kingdom in 2011
by Krupt Publishing

www.thejunctionchurch.com

ISBN 978-0-9569471-0-9

Produced by The Choir Press

Dedication

This book is dedicated to my beautiful wife and gorgeous kids.

You are the inspiration of my life and I love you more than words can express.

Also to my Parents who passed away just 17 days apart. They were the original warriors of independence and gave us children hope, faith and freedom.

About the Author

Kevin Upton is the Senior Pastor of 'The Junction Church' Aberdeen, Church planter and trainer and also speaks widely across Europe. He is a husband, a Dad, an artist and illustrator, loves swimming and er wait ... let me think, oh yeah he is also apparently an Author. Heaven help us all!

Kevin has a funny and relevant style which helps people see the reality of their lives they lead and encourages all to build into the local church.

Contents

People I couldn't have written this book without ...

Pastor Abby Aitken of the Point COC. You are truly insane and I cannot thank you enough for your editorial input and humour which helped me keep my edge.

Grace Cook. You're a rock and an amazing editor and your help was invaluable.

Nathanael Tingle. You truly are the world's greatest nerd. Thank you for spotting the mistakes again and again (hope you got them all.)

Pastor Claus Hermansen of Connect Church in Hobro, Denmark. Thank you for spotting the mistakes that Nathanael missed (clearly Nathanael didn't get them all).

Miriam Gardiner. I can't remember what you did now, but you work for me so you must have done something. Thank you.

Nelly Jaka and Hatty Minty. Thank you for all the admin and organisation. Your reward is in heaven. So speak to Jesus about pay day OK?

Foreword

The Dangerous World of Stuff and Things is wickedly outrageous! Author Kevin Upton is also one of the funniest people I've ever had the privilege to meet. Kevin is insightful, articulate, and has the ability to see things from a totally different perspective. *The Dangerous World of Stuff and Things* is a book that will make you laugh and then cry. You just have to read this book – you'll get so much out of it and be very glad you did!

Tom Rawls Lead Pastor of Proclaimers, Norwich
Author of *Relentless: A Renaissance Theology for the 21st Century Church* which is available on Amazon

Kevin Upton has a way with words. Like the great Adrian Plass, he has a keen eye for observing the small stuff of life along with the absurd, the blazingly obvious and the thoughts we quickly and quietly ignore due to their politically incorrect overtones.

Kevin doesn't just observe them; he has a way of expressing them that is both incredibly refreshing and humorously revealing. In a Christian world of predictability and 'many blessings to you,' Kevin delights us with both playful description and articulate observations.

He says a lot of stuff we always thought wasn't quite right to say. And for that we thank him.

Dave Gilpin Senior Pastor of Hope City Church, Sheffield
Minor Christian Celebrity
Author of *Sacred Cows Make Great BBQs* and a number of excellent books which are available on Amazon

Kevin Upton needs help! He needs help is so many ways there is not enough time to tell it here, read this book, you will see what I mean, he is in trouble and needs a doctor and drugs.

But seriously ...

I like Kevin Upton a lot because he is slightly iconoclastic, by that I mean, if you have any idols he will challenge them, confront them, and push them over! This books does that in many ways, and on so many levels. If you have any idols or things you like to protect, this book, hunts them down and in a captivatingly funny way, destroys them. More power to

Scott Wilson
Author of *The G Factor* and a number of excellent books on church leadership

Often Ministers are portrayed as being humourless, boring creatures lacking the ability to even raise a smile in the funniest of times.

In his book "The dangerous world of stuff and things", Kevin Upton shatters this myth, causing you to laugh at situations you have experienced whilst encouraging you to look at and deal with the Elephant in the room.

Neil Cameron
Senior Pastor, New Hope Church, Peterhead

Disclaimer:

While the text within this book describes the lives of people that I may have interacted with, I want it to be known that in no way could that person be you. All names, age, sex, profession and religion have been changed to protect those who have a lot of stuff and things going on in their lives. If at anytime you feel I might be talking about you, please realise I'm only talking about the human condition in a pluralistic and generalized manner befitting a Christian book. Amen.

With that in mind, please read the book all the way to the end so that its humour and truth can change your thinking, if only by a little.

As you read I will take you on my journey as I have traversed the crazy world of developing relationships and building lives. The stories all rotate around a central theme that if read through to the conclusion will help you understand what a world of excuses we create.

All of us have stuff and things going on in our lives and the following chapters have been written to help identify how they manifest in our lives.

The process of the book will take you humouredly to one conclusion ... Well I can't tell you can I? You have to read the book.

CHAPTER 1

Losing control

He that is good for making excuses is seldom good for anything else – Benjamin Franklin

It was 9am on Sunday morning as I passed Calvin on the stairs. He slumped into the church looking like a battered haggis. Clearly, his life was dealing him some hard blows – his shoulders hung like they had just fallen out of their sockets, his normally bland clothes were also seriously un-kempt, his hair – well I don't want to make you nauseous, not so soon anyway! Our ever buoyant welcome team put on their bravest effort to make Calvin's day special. Margaret, our wise and cheery steward, put her arm around him and led him downstairs and out of sight of visitors (*well, first impressions count!*).

"What's been going on in your life then, Calvin?" Margaret enquired.

"Oh, I'm just going through stuff", he mumbled.

His depressed – and depressing – tone emphasising the apparent awfulness of this particular strain of 'stuff', so bad it had completely destroyed his relationship with showers, deodorant, soap, toothpaste and particularly water of any temperature or source. This 'stuff' was clearly very nasty and had a lot to answer for – whatever it was?!

I tore myself away from the richly roasted coffee aroma of the café bar and entered the main auditorium. There was a buzz of last minute activity as people ran back and forth preparing for 10.30 kick off. I passed our media operator Linda as she was rushing with much focus to stick a battery into something or someone.

"Hey, Linda how's you" I casually ask, as I head to my 'guaranteed' front row seat (based upon the principle of 'you park, you preach!')

"Huh!" She spits back at me, her frizzy orange hair making her look a bit like an orange on a cocktail stick. I look back at her surprised and, frankly, wanting a nicer answer!

"It's … it's just 'things' … you know 'things'!" She quickly added.

"WOW!" I mouth to myself as I park my rear on my seat. "Whatever these 'stuff' and 'things' are – they're sounding pretty dangerous to me … "

As the service kicks off and the place comes to life, I glance around to see the ever reliable late-comers doing their predictable 'tiptoe dance'.

Why do they do that? It's pumping 105 decibels and we have a carpet with a pile depth that you could lose a small child in … well, a piece of Lego at least – and still the 'tiptoe tango' is essential for every persistent late-comer, coupled with the flustered look of "I'm so unavoidably and justifiably late due to 'stuff' and 'things' … "

Our lives work because we have set disciplines or habits in place; that when fitted together, determine whether we get up in time to be nice to our neighbour and to be presentable at work. Then 'stuff' and 'things' happen and we can't even organise putting our pants on the right way!

At this point, our individual characters dictate what will happen next (not so much with the pants, more in regards to the 'stuff' and 'things'). Calvin became depressed, Linda became stressed, and those who tiptoe through life become blame-shifters. Basically they've lost control. They're out of control and not so much 'loving it' as 'excusing it'!

Calvin's Stuff

Calvin is going through 'stuff'. These are issues which he is choosing to keep to himself; he knows what they are, but is not telling. So he names the issues 'stuff' – 'stuff' is therefore something bad, kind of like the activity of the devil, but less super-spiritual. His reason for keeping 'stuff' a secret serves several purposes: It keeps it mystical and out of reach of prying pastors who may have something to say about his life.

If it is not the devil, then others looking on and praying are not sure how to help; meanwhile, the devil's admiring what a great job is being done without him lifting a finger. So as the old saying says (if you say it back to front) "if it is broke don't fix it"!

The big secret about 'stuff' and where it gets its power is never actually mentioning what it is. If that happens, it's all over. Everyone will know what the issue is and it won't be 'stuff' because, well, it's just a word and people will actually know what to do about it! Of course once they do then it will be mended, and where would Calvin be then? Healed of course, but no longer able to attract the attention on which he had thrived.

Most things remain 'stuff'. It's the first law of 'stuff' and 'things', avoiding the details or the specific. So naturally the second law is: have an issue that can't be fixed! That's where 'stuff' fits perfectly; if it can't be named it can't be fixed.

Now Calvin can gain sympathy from unsuspecting believers eager to outwork their new found faith message on a prime candidate. Calvin is happy to have attention as he will have these merry faith-suckers running around him for weeks. They will pray for him, buy him things, treat him well, feed him – but Calvin's lips are sealed. 'Stuff' is the enemy – and a well camouflaged enemy at that. When 'stuff' is revealed, then the real answers appear quite obvious.

Many of us fall into this story either in the role of Calvin or sometimes as the sucker that wants to help, but the devil is in the detail and it's the detail that reveals Calvin's true heart. He doesn't want to admit that his lifestyle (decisions, self confession, and ungodly belief) is really the enemy. Calvin is out of control but the trouble is he is the only one with the controls!

I make a point of asking one of the leaders to see Calvin as I think its time we nail this 'stuff' once and for all. My ever ready and always serving leader sighs with great disappointment. He obviously has been tricked by this dangerous sympathy-devouring 'stuff' once before.

"Clive" I say, with the sort of voice that only pastors

are allowed to use. "Clive, it's time to nail Calvin and get him to face some issues and you're the man for the job."

This time my tone is enthusiastic and empowering. I'm hoping Clive will feel special at this moment and take on this rather awkward job with great excitement. My hope isn't entirely lost. Clive isn't stupid but neither is he unwilling. (I have great leaders in my church; people who not only lead but know how to get people free). Calvin will go on a coaching programme, a short decisive course over a few weeks to start with, teaching him how to deal with set issues in his life and gain the control in his life that he never had before.

Linda's 'Things'

Linda has 'things', a sibling to 'stuff' and equally nasty. She is flapping, stressed and out of control, her enemy is 'things'. 'Things' have been going on in her life for a while. She has college 'things' and boy 'things', family 'things', money 'things', sometimes there are clothes 'things' and hair 'things', there are even church 'things' – JUST 'THINGS'!

Now these 'things' you can't easily describe; whatever they are, it's just not good. What is worse is that these 'things' sometimes all arrive together to make a 'thing day'!

Now of course, Linda has a way of dealing with it, and usually in a very disagreeable manner (most unlike the John Maxwell book she's just read on the 'Power of Influence,') but of course all this is understandable because remember she's going through you know what!

The first act of dealing with the avalanche of 'things' is for Linda to let everyone know in as many dramatic ways imaginable that 'things' are happening, such as when she was rushing from the toilets into worship with her dress tucked into her knickers! This is another perfect example of the bad and uncontrollable 'things' that just seem to keep happening to her. Just like 'stuff', 'things' are a way to excuse being out of control without facing the true facts. Linda is simply living carelessly (even in the loo!). Her life consists of careless relationships and a careless lifestyle. Living out of control empowers 'things', so as long as she can blame it on 'things', what does it matter?

It is easier to be careless and blame it on 'things' than it is to take time and make sure that you look after the different areas of your life; such as with your friends, college work, church, money and clothing.

A little time taken to be nice to her parents and friends and a little more thought about how much money was going out compared to coming in would set Linda on a path of control and 'things' would disappear like bubbles in the wind. Linda is young and has the opportunity to change relatively pain free. I say that with gritted teeth. I'm in my 40's and change for some reason is increasingly difficult to deal with in me. I am hoping all my young people can see what issues they really have while they are young enough to deal with them and make quality choices about how they build their lives. Sadly, I have too many people who tell stories of 'things' that have dogged their lives and their greatest regret is that they never faced it when they could.

Blame Shifters

Blame shifters are great possessors of 'stuff' and 'things'. Their lives are not always like Calvin's or Linda's. They may have a grip on life and are very concerned by what others think. No careless comments or throw away lines. No sales technique to get others to feel sorry for them. These can be good people with great potential.

I remember one such lady who had regularly attended our church for a couple of years. With a successful career in the oil industry she had gained great favour in the city, was well respected by other churches and well known for wise counsel. However, she was a 'tiptoer.' An original and classic latecomer with choreography that could be envied by Michael Jackson! With a position similar to that of "Thriller", on tiptoes, body tilted forward, arms stretched out in front (which I can only assume is to touch the chair quicker than the rest of the body therefore not being as late!) Something about this position allows the individual involved to believe that they are now invisible to the naked eye?!

In this instance, I am baffled at the effort involved in coming late. There is no strict time policy at church, you can come in when you like, but still the great choreographed routine must be done. However, with a plush carpeted floor and worship so loud that those in front of the speakers have nosebleeds and new hairstyles, why bother with the effort of the dancing entrance, just sit down. But to this focused woman it was essential.

To the more super-spiritual posse in the congregation

this was, of course, a prophetic dance and needed to have agreement in the form of a warfare/worship/weirdo conga. Before long, the army of prophetic dancers steer around the church with the infamous tiptoe lady as the front bumper bar. I am also convinced I can hear, under the noise of the worship, a sewing machine churning out flags and banners . . .?!! As is inevitable, the space at the front (which can barely hold a fold back monitor) cannot withhold the whooping, weaving mass of women; and to our shock and horror, before we can say something rude in tongues, we're a dancer down. Not any old dancer, but our tiptoe bumper bar, in what seems to happen as a blur of slow motion. Within milliseconds we have a self appointed intercessor ministering deliverance to our tiptoe lady, who is wailing in pain as she ironically appears to have broken her toes . . . All she wanted to do was tiptoe in late without me seeing her.

After the service, and recovery of all those who were maimed in the chaos, I see her hiding behind a rather overweight man. When I eventually catch her eye and smile sympathetically, she walks towards me apologising for the commotion blaming 'stuff' and 'things' for being late and how she's never going to be late like that again! But we both know she will! She's a blame shifter and 'stuff' and 'things' are the reason for her disarray.

What goes on in her life is rather a mystery, She is generally very organised and well presented but 'stuff' and 'things' such as wanting her mother to get saved and being driven by fear of situations she cannot change, mean that instead of being the minister and woman of influence in the situation, she becomes part of the problem and from the earlier carry on attracts problems for me ... I hate 'stuff' and 'things'.

Fear interrupts her routine, unsettles her plans and disrupts her timetable. She cannot admit to this as she is too 'successful', therefore her life becomes a slave to an excuse of 'stuff' and 'things'. She becomes a blame shifter and a tiptoer, literally and very dangerously! Her life in the secular world is controlled and dependable, but when it comes to God she has issues. Her faith also reveals her heart. She controls because she is afraid. Yet even if you can control everything around you, you cannot control yourself. Your heart will betray you. What this lady has become is miles short of where she wanted to be, and she knows it. Whether she will gain control of her private life will not depend on whether she can extend the borders of control she has in the workplace but whether she can admit to being weak, afraid and unable to cope with her family. This admittance will give her more control than any positive confession ever could.

CHAPTER 2

The thing about me

He who excuses himself, accuses himself. –
Gabriel Meurier

Things happen to me that others can explain but I cannot. To me it's simply a huge part of my life, which provides me with my mad and hectic adventures and my wife with yet another story to laugh at. My wife Cheryl is an angel, but she has a dark side. She laughs helplessly at my mishaps and will remind herself of them at different times of the day or night. I could be just drifting off to sleep when I am snatched from my slumber with her giggling uncontrollably about something that happened 20 years ago. Her favourite is before we were married. I was in a hurry to get out of the house and I shut my head in the door. I still have no idea how it happened but there I was – my head squished between door and frame like an orange in a juicer. Then there was the time when the kids were small and I turned the bedroom light off. Cheryl had already gone to bed and I remembered I'd left my water in the kitchen, I turned and somehow head

butted the doorframe so hard I split my eyebrow open
and blood started pouring everywhere. I needed to go
to A&E for stitches but as the kids were fast asleep in
bed and it seemed too much bother to wake them, I sat
in front of the electric fire in the lounge nursing my
face, while Cheryl laughed like a hyena. She has this
ability to be incredibly sweet and caring, while taking
personal delight in my little accidents.

My darling wife makes me feel loved and very
humbled all at the same time. Being humbled is a
particular gift of mine, its my ... thing ... Recently
while travelling in a 1st class train carriage from North
Jutland to Copenhagen airport, I became aware there
was a lot of activity around me; it transpired that the
train had developed a fault and we had to change trains
at the next station. This information was given to me
by a caring Danish man, who could see I was
completely clueless to the situation. Now I have
discovered that while travelling on public transport in
foreign lands you are best to make friends with the
locals. They are the ones who will help you when
things don't go according to plan. So my friendly local
informed me of the need to change trains as the one
we were travelling on had developed a fault. I got ready
to disembark throwing bags over my shoulder and
scanning the area of my carriage in case I had left
something behind. The train glided smoothly into
Arhus station most unlike a busted train.

I stood behind my friendly local and decided that
I would follow him as he would know which
platform to catch the replacement train from and
where to stand when it arrived. (In Denmark you
must know where your seat is as the trains do not

always allow you to walk from one end to the other). As the doors of the train whooshed open my kindly local shot off like a man guilty of some wicked crime. "Flip!" I exclaimed to myself, "This guy must know something I don't." I shot behind him passing anxious travellers hanging around the platforms looking for their train to come up on the screens. He ran up the stairs avoiding the overcrowded escalators. I was going to have to hurry; I had no idea which platform the train would leave from and guessed that if I lost him I was stuffed! I grabbed my suitcase, slung my hand luggage over my shoulder and bolted after him. We raced 20 paces apart, tearing past small children un-tethered from their weary parents. My mind raced, "Where the hell is this train? Why is this man going so fast and why is he going to the front doors of the station?" The cold stark realisation that I had chosen to follow the wrong kindly local began to dawn on me. My legs took long slow exaggerated strides as I tried looking around for someone who might know what to do. The station was heavy with ignorant carefree passengers. The notice board flashed infor-mation in Danish which I could read, if I had a spare 45 minutes and an interpreter!

I looked wildly to my left and right, my eyes began to bulge as my heart rate, already working overtime from the obviously foolish dash up from the platform, began to thump into heart attack gear. There was only one thing I could do. I raced at break-neck speed to catch up with my 'friendly local.' I caught him by surprise as he passed through the automatic glass doors. His once friendly eyes looked at me as if I was a complete idiot. Before I could splutter out my request, he calmly stated, "The train you need is on the opposite platform from where you came." He then turned and walked away without another word. I felt like I'd just had a personal message from the grim reaper!

I spun around and stared down the long Victorian style station. On the left side lay a variety of shops, ticket booths and cafes. To the right high above the plethora of stairwells jutting out into the open space were the platform numbers, not that they were any help. Might as well have been in Japanese for all the help they were to me. I hadn't a clue which platform I had come from and each stairwell was horribly identical, bar the platform number high above. They silently mocked me as I charged back in the general direction from whence I thought I came.

Missing my train would mean inevitably missing my plane, which would mean being away from Cheryl for even longer. Although my trips are normally only 3-4 days, I can never wait to get home. I'm still a country boy at heart. Give me a farmhouse out in the sticks, a few cows, sheep, horses and a gun to shoot them with, and I'm a happy man! However, the Lord has chosen to use me in a very different capacity and who am I to argue?

I throw my unfit body (as I had so dramatically recently discovered) down an escalator. There is no time for traditional Danish conversation and politeness. Assuming I have returned to the scene of the crime, I thundered over to the only obvious stationary train, barging through the patient crowds who are trying to alight their transportation.

I spot a person in a luminous jacket and lurch in

front of them – despite the fact they are giving instructions to an elderly lady. My earnestness demanding their attention is met with cold silence and indifferent eyes. I realise at this moment that station guards around the world are trained by the KGB and have the ability to dislocate your spine with a single stare. I shrink back feeling somewhat like I did as a child at school who desperately needed permission to leave the classroom for a pee.

I fidget from one foot to the other waiting my turn. Eventually the guard nods in my direction and assures me this is the correct train to Copenhagen airport. Still wound up and tensed by the whole experience, I leap on without checking the carriage number. I have a reserved seat in carriage 21 and suddenly realise that I don't know if I am on the right part of the train! I rotate maniacally, blurting out, "Is this carriage 21?" My panic stops me from looking 12 inches above my head to an illuminated sign simply stating 21! Thumping through the carriage, panting heavily, I begin to notice my heart has shifted places and is now firmly placed in my neck. My seat placidly awaits me as if none of this ever happened, but I know it did, as now do most of my fellow travelling companions. I want the train to move on, but it doesn't – it just sits there making me realise that all that panic was for nothing.

I had been humbled once again. How it happens, I have no idea. It's just one of those things! Now, you would think that having just been through such trauma, I would be more careful. So you would think . . .

I arrived at the airport in plenty of time and checked

in. Airports are pretty much the same the world over. Only the differing levels of grumpy staff setting them apart. On the scale of 1 – 10, (if 1 was mildly indifferent and 10 were raging thugs) the U.S. would be a 9 while Denmark would score a 3. The UK would be a 6 or 7. However, for the weary traveller, the whole experience is pretty much frustratingly the same. As I gathered my belongings from security, I decided to get my wife a present from the tax free shops. Now, to the untraveled reader, these are not to be confused with profit free shops. They might not have tax added to the sale but they sure have a healthy mark up.

I find a suitable 'girly' shop and purchase a beautiful bag. I am now very pleased with myself and know I'm bound to get a big snog for my 'thoughtfulness'!! I decide to treat myself to a large cinnamon dolce latte. As I'm waiting for my gate to be called this wave of fear comes over me. I'm not sure specifically where this fear is coming from; is someone, somewhere about to start sticking pins in a voodoo doll called Kevin? Have I left something? I feel like I've left something, but can't imagine what.

I start frisking myself maniacally: pens, chewing gum, sachets of ketchup, receipts from 2003, wallet, phone, ipod, spare change. What on earth am I missing? I retrace my steps in my head, security check, girly shop ... aagh, the gorgeous bag I'm going to get snogged for! I run through the waiting lounge out to the duty free shopping area. I return to the last place I remember being (the currency exchange) and stand in a queue. I really don't have time to wait, so once again I bounce and hover like a child that needs a wee but says they don't. I try putting on the most pleading childlike eyes I can find, but am aware that the over-all effect is lost on the recipient and I end up looking like I have escaped from my carer (who has a special white jacket with tie up sleeves just for me). Eventually I get to the desk; the girl looks at me and pulls my bag up like a rabbit from a hat. I smile sheepishly and return to the waiting lounge.

The next 45 minutes went by without an event or drama. My flight was called and I went through my gate and waited for the bus that would take us to the plane. Having done this journey many times, I have expertly calculated where to stand so as to be the first off the bus and on to the plane. All this has to be done in one smooth action as it would look very infantile if you were seen trying to get ahead of everyone else; which of course is exactly what I'm trying to do. Obviously, there are several other well travelled men who have all worked out the same strategy. The resulting exit to the bus is a very constrained march to the plane steps, where grown men in suits are walking as fast as they can and trying to look indifferent all at the same time. Everyone wants to be crowned 1st and no one wants to be seen trying. Running is clearly out of the question. It's all about position, pace and lots of practice.

On this occasion, however, the unofficial race to be first on the plane is ruined by an uneducated woman who had the cheek to run! She is met with several sets of disapproving male eyes. I'm shoved back into fourth place and feel quite disgruntled that I have put in all that effort and I'm not even in a medal position

I quickly realise on entering the plane that something is missing yet again. No need to do the mental gymnastics this time, it's my flipping bag! The trouble is, it is now a quarter of a mile away on the other side of the airport, this is not a time to give up. I turn in a bull-like fashion pushing against 150 passengers coming the other way. I realise shouting manically will help so I start blurting out, "My bag, er, its black … Jasper Conran … back at the gate … on a chair near the door." I'm not sure how the pilot interpreted the message, but by the time they bolted me back into my chair and all the other passengers were seated the bag was safely back in my hands.

I receive it with a knowing smile, as others around squint their eyes in that fashion when one is plotting something murderous. I don't care anymore; I have been through too many 'things' in one day. I lean back heavily into my seat and close my eyes, my bag still clenched tightly in my fist. I try and sleep while I wonder whatever is next …?

CHAPTER 3

A Woman's thing

Two wrongs don't make a right, but they make a good excuse – Thomas Szasz

1 – The Angry Rhino

Ethel marched into my office like an angry rhino. She always charged everywhere huffing, puffing, frowning, and occasionally snorting as if she was hunting down someone. This never portrayed her actual mood and it was obviously her default setting. She thumped her bag onto my table and declared with a deep Aberdonian accent that "God had been speaking to her all night." I shuddered as I began to wonder what was coming. There are several alarms going off in my head despite the fact I'm doing my best to remain calm and 'pastor like'. My first concern was that due to it being 'God' that had kept her up all night, and not an angel or demon or fairy, what was coming next could not be reasoned with, debated or even queried. After all, you can't argue with God! My second concern was that she had been up all night talking to God . . . This normally meant that it was of particular importance ('the earth turning to vaporous smoke' type of importance).

Ethel comes from a long line of intercessors who have specialized their prayer ministry to receiving words at certain times of the day. A mid-morning word was of exhortation to a younger lady who needed to be taught 'things.' A word in the evening was spoken in hushed tones and usually involved sexually immoral 'stuff' and a Jezebel spirit. But a word in the night; oh now that is altogether different! This is a word which determines the destiny of cities, changes nations and most definitely puts fear up the pastor!!

My third concern was related to the first two, but was coming from somewhere else … It's my 'bad person alarm.' When this one goes off, I have to be especially restrained as I can hear myself saying just the most terrible things, like, "What the heck were you doing up all night?", "Didn't God make night for sleeping?", "Were you keeping company with vampires again?" and "How come God informs you of nation changing events and all I get is 'I love you my son'?" (More importantly, which little rodent in my office let this damn woman in here in the first place!!?)

Ethel clutched her bosoms in a vice like grip. It was going to be a long story ("Please Jesus let the phone ring, let there be a death in the church, a sales call, where are the J.W's when you need them? ….").

I hated it when she clutched her bosoms – I have mental scars from my childhood because of a lady who was just like this. My mind sent me back to those times with Mrs Higgins who was a large lady from the strict Baptist chapel where we attended church. She sang hideously out of tune and also had a son who was completely mad due to her continued mothering. She just wouldn't let him go, so the poor man, who was well into his 40's and had been very intelligent, just went off his rocker. Every so often Mrs Higgins felt the need to mother someone younger and that victim was me. She would sneak up and grab me from behind, and suck me into her enormous bosoms. There was no point in screaming as I couldn't be heard; I could hardly breathe as I was jammed into her cleavage like a hot dog in a bun! Each mammary gland I swear was the size of a small horse; no man should die in such a terrible way, let alone a 10 year old boy ...

I phased back in to see Ethel tightening her gripped arms around her ample bosom ("Oh help, this is getting worse"). She had been ranting on for some time now about angels, forces of darkness, the anti-Christ spirit, and wrestling them ("In mud, I wonder? ... Shut up bad pastor" I said to myself) and gaining a great victory where the spirit was finally able to deliver His word. I waited with bated breath – more because she also smelled of onions rather than anticipation.

"LET MY WOMEN GO!"

"Crumbs", I say to myself, "She had to wrestle all night for four words? I'm sure glad I'm not an 'intercessor.' How long would you have to wrestle to get a really long word? You could die in the process! Now call me old fashioned but didn't she just rip off Moses?"

"Let my women go?" I enquire, "Any particular woman or all of them?" I know I'm treading on thin ice. Ethel is a feminist intercessor and the bases for all complaints are founded on the fact that all women are constrained and bound in the church by the piggery of male pastors, leaders and elders, etc. Of course Ethel is the self appointed mouth- piece and servant of the Lord.

"I'm sorry, Ethel you've lost me. I don't understand."
Of course I did understand – I understood all too well
– but to spend time working through what this woman
was going on about was not worth the pain. Anyway, I
had an appointment with the gym in 5 minutes and I
had to wrap up this prophetic word and get out of
here.

"Oh!" she said, lifting her bosom so high I nearly lost
sight of her face, "Of course you wouldn't understand! It's
a 'woman thing.' I'm off to see your wife, is she around?"

A 'woman thing'? No one has a thing! Not a woman,
not a man. Now for ease of conversation and for
fluency of speech we use the word 'thing' where a
word or object is difficult to describe or rather vague.
However, Ethel was using it for something altogether
different. The 'thing' had become the property of the
female race and therefore utterly out of reach of men;
who are, of course, completely insensitive, dominating,
controlling and utterly stupid.

No one really knew Ethel, she was a closed book.
She dressed in a tweed skirt lined with sandpaper,
jacket to match with pockets everywhere, not so much
as a speck of make up and a hair cut your sergeant
major would be proud of. She spoke and lived like a
woman who had been abused and broken by some
man in her life who should have known better. Of
course that was a lifetime ago. As far as Ethel was
concerned she had been healed, empowered and
commissioned by the Holy Ghost to set women free
and intercede for the nations.

Now Ethel was empowering the 'woman thing'. It is
of course the great unknown, as no woman has been

able to describe what a 'woman's thing' is; as if she had, it wouldn't be called a 'thing' anymore, but something much more descriptive and confidence boosting. She wanted to let me know that women have something that men just wouldn't or couldn't understand. This is very important as it helps her to maintain her own self identity and behaviour toward others.

Ethel is really a very intimidated and discouraged woman. Her self loathing is only matched by her hatred of men who have robbed from her life itself. Of course this poor self image tells very big lies. So when I question her, it's taken as a complete rejection of not only her but all women; as she is the representation of women kind. My rejection of her is seen in the same light as the hurt and abuse she received many years previously. The ministry she has developed and grown up in is an outworking of women's hurt. She can do business with God in a world where there is no real interaction with man. In a normal world a woman would most likely share her life with a man giving him heart and colour, feeling and expression and being counter balanced with the pale tones of logic and childlike obsession, but that is not a world where Ethel can afford to go. So she expresses her feminine needs in the unrestrained world of spiritual experience, pulling her soul into fanciful pictures, overdone colours and emotional words. This is, of course, God speaking to her. In some senses, she is not wrong: the Spirit will not withhold Himself from a desperate soul, but a wounded soul will colour their world with the shades of pain that rest over their eyes, changing the true picture of this world to one that fits their life experience.

My hope for Ethel is never realised. If I could speak to her in a pastoral context where her defences are down, I may be able to speak to her hurt and bring the healing balm that only a man could bring. Her fight and anguish has so dominated her life for more than 50 years that it seems she will not stop long enough to see that her 'woman thing' is in fact the isolation she feels because of the abuse she received when she was young. It was then that her femininity was stolen, her identity crushed and her destiny confused. Ethel's character determined what she would become from there on in. A strong fighter by nature will go to war against such injustice but the war can never be won. You cannot right this wrong, you cannot undo the past. The only hope is found in Matthew 6:12: 'Lord forgive me my debts as I forgive my debtors,' but this is not so easily found. Forgiveness is so often and so easily quoted, but considering how important it is and the priority with which God places it in His word, it seems so elusive and difficult to find. Ethel never allows me close enough to the real woman hiding behind the rage.

The saddest part of all this is that it is her 'thing' that has ultimately robbed her true destiny and effectiveness from the church. We will never know what we have missed in Ethel, because we never saw her true colours. The church will always be poorer for never knowing a woman with such fighting spirit. I can only imagine what could have been.

2 - The Invisible Mouse

Rachel sat quiet and unnoticed in the reception area. Ethel had freely marched straight past her despite the fact Rachel had been waiting patiently for one of the pastors to be made available. She had hoped for one of our ladies but not having made an appointment it was unlikely that Cheryl or Catriona was going to be available. So Rachel sat quiet as a mouse and uncomplaining, waited for someone to speak to. This was classic Rachel. She would soak up all the stress of what was going on around her but never say a word. Everyone loved her because she was so easy, never a bother and always willing to help. She was never going to be a star; in fact it truly was best to keep her behind the scenes. Not just because she had one of those awkward postures that seem to make every limb and joint move in the wrong direction whenever she came into contact with someone (especially a man), but also because she had a face like a rabbit caught between the headlights of a moving truck.

"I'm sorry, Rachel", I said, giving her one of those looks that said "Hell, that woman is a pain in the neck", but Rachel never took me on. I don't think she even noticed, her gaze rarely left the ground when in the company of pastors. She probably could have told me where all the missing pens and paperclips were with the length of time that the poor girl had waited and closely examined every inch of carpet!

"Is Cheryl around?" she blurted, and then for some unknown reason her left shoulder lurched up while her head sort of twitched and rotated on her neck. I often wondered how anyone could possibly do that without needing immediate medical attention.

"I'm sorry Rachel, she's busy at present but I'm here with the office staff", I wave my arm in a sweeping action behind me to show our poor frightened girl that despite the fact she may have to speak to a man there are several friendly female faces close enough to come to the rescue should she need their assistance.

"Oh", she hesitates. This time, her long skinny frame squirms in her oversized coat. Her eyes roll toward me but quickly find their place back on the floor. "Er", she starts again "it's a 'woman thing'."

Now I'm in a dilemma. There are some things that women have that are not what a man wants or needs to know or to even think about. Now, of course, these things are in fact real issues but a woman is just not going to share these issues with any blockhead of a man – even if he is the pastor! Yet I was not convinced that she has 'woman things' which she needs help with, but in fact something else completely different was going on.

I look at her this time not as a Pastor but as a dad. I have fathered many people in my life over and above the children I have at home. "You're lonely, aren't you?"

She rotates thirty degrees, twists her head like an owl and finally caves in and tears roll down her long, pale cheeks. Rachel might be on the odder side of odd but she is also the sweetest girl you would ever wish to know. I find it hard not to cry with her.

Rachel's 'woman thing' was really loneliness. She called it a 'thing' so as not to reveal the pain. Once I had spoken the word 'lonely' everything was let loose! Rachel wanted to keep everything neat in a tidy chat with an understanding female she felt safe with. She wanted to talk about praying more and reading the Bible and having worship playing in the house so as to keep her spirit strong. However, that was not the issue. Rachel's issue is not at all like Ethel, she has never been hurt, abused or anything like that, but simply, she hated her appearance so much she could not come to terms with herself relating to the opposite sex even on a perfectly normal friendship basis.

Rachel, at this point, needed not words of advice on how to deal with this thing that dominated her world, not how to look and dress like the 32 year old she really was or place lipstick on her see-through lips. None of these things are of value at a moment like this. Rachel needed a dad who could place value on her for being her. Her real dad had been a tall intellectual and had failed to see her need for love and encouragement through her teenage years. He was a good man, but just didn't know how to connect.

I glanced over my shoulder to catch the eye of one of my ladies in the office, who very quickly came over with a box of tissues. Now Rachel needed a hug, not just from a man who she could trust implicitly but from a father figure in her life that would begin to heal the brokenness of her femininity. While Rachel sobbed on my new shirt ("Why did I wear a new shirt today?" I thought to myself,) my assistant fed her tissues and prayed quietly, soothing away the pent up emotion that had filled her heart.

Women's 'things' are very dangerous, but sometimes I have to dare to venture in and discover what they really are. For most they are a cloak to cover the issues they dare not face themselves. Whatever your 'thing' is, don't blame your husband, your father or even men in general. Instead, become a woman in your own right, content and satisfied with yourself and not a victim to the car crash of interaction with men who give all of us a bad name.

CHAPTER 4

Single Simon Simpleton

Every vice has its excuse ready. Publilius Syrus

The engine roared with life as we caught some air over a small humped bridge in the country roads of Aberdeenshire. It was a beautiful winter day. The sun was low on the horizon; leafless trees looking like special edition twiglets stood between field and mountain. The horizon was disappearing into pastel shades of purple.

Unfortunately, though, we were not here to breathe country air and reflect on the beauty of our surroundings; though I certainly would have preferred right at this moment to spend some much needed time with Cheryl and take stock of the glorious country that God had called us to.

No, for my sins, I was sharing what Simon called a 'pleasant country jaunt' while we chatted about his continual single status that had haunted him since the age of 16. I on the other hand called it "a ride into hell". Simon had a 3 litre bright yellow 1979 Ford

Capri, complete with fake leather seat covers that were so badly and desperately stretched over the seats they would have looked more at home in a combine harvester. And yes, as you're sitting there wondering if he had a magic tree – (he did) – a VANILLA one that smelt of baby sick and gone off milk. Added to the special driving gloves and glasses, this was just the finishing touch needed to ensure the diabolic trip was as awkward as possible.

Now for those of you who, by the mercy of God, have not been defiled by the activities of such a 44 year old single man, a 'country jaunt' is not what it suggests, and the purchase of such a high powered car is not actually to have the ability to drag cars out of ditches. No, this is for another type of pulling power completely! As his desperation for a mate had reached breaking point, Simon was taking matters into his own hands. Despite 28 years of wrinkly-old intercessors proclaiming, declaring and prophesying, or even speed-dating in the church hall, nothing had had the desired result. The Lord had clearly 'shown' him the 21yr old blonde woman he was to marry and it was obvious (to absolutely nobody BUT Simon) that this would only come to pass with the purchase of a bright yellow car!

All you beautiful, single, 21 year old blonde ladies are in danger of being enticed into this magnet of passion; where you will drape your gorgeous, svelte body, appropriately under-dressed, on the fake leather passenger seating that has 30 years of smoke worn into it by fat, old men leering over their fantasies …. . I mean future wives. Your name is waiting to be placed next to his on the stone chipped windscreen; of course he hopes you won't notice the chipped screen and has placed a sticker stating he shops at 'Lidl' to cover this flaw in his otherwise perfect classic.

The car suddenly slides to a halt as Simon Spots a buzzard making a kill. Buzzards are quite common in this part of the country and are sometimes mistaken as golden eagles by the tourists. He gets out his new 12 mega pixel camera, leaps from the car like a 10 year old boy and snaps some shots of this magnificent killing machine. I'm surprised. Just when you think you have a person checked out, they surprise you. I like this part of pastoring, discovering new depths in a man you first thought was quite shallow. Suddenly I discover he loves ornithology. 'Mmm' I muse, 'Simon has interests more interesting than bright yellow cars' ... of course, I'm not cynical enough to think that maybe he just likes all types of birds!

However, my impression of him was quickly reinforced when he tried climbing back into the car. Capris are fairly low and Simon is fairly wide in his back bumper area! He has developed a skill of bum first, legs last, which involves sticking a huge shiny leather clad backside straight toward my face. Just at the moment I think daylight has been blotted out forever, he swings it down into the old fake leather seat, swings his stubby legs back in and lets out a huge puff of pent-up air that had been caught in his rib cage. It's at this moment that I realise what my wife is going on about with men and their bottoms. "Unless a man has an amazingly firm bottom he should abstain from leather trousers." I could hear her voice and also imagine her disgust at what I had just experienced. Probably better I don't mention it; she would make me shower before tea time just to make sure I didn't pick up any impurities. I shudder, "That was way too close … think I might have a shower anyway … maybe use some of that exfoliation stuff just to be safe … " I muse.

"Put on a bit of weight Simon?" I enquire with that sort of tone that says "Ha ha, you're a fat pig", in a really jolly way!

"No no" he says quite adamantly while the trousers heave under the pressure of an expanding waistline coupled with an awkward seating position.

I begin to squint, his top trouser button is under so much strain it looks like it could fly off at any moment, ricochet off the dashboard and give me a third eye socket! I decide to look at the scenery from the passenger window and make light conversation of the beautiful countryside (although that button could now become impaled in my ear hole). Now I wish I had those pink fluffy ear muffs that were hand-me-downs from my sister that my mum made me wear to school.

He finally caves in, having completely ignored all my other cues to talk about being single and needing a good woman. "I want a wife", he blurts, then quickly proceeds to explain how long he had been single and why there were no ladies in the church, and that the ones who he knew were all too old, and he would have to go to other places around the world, and on and on it went until finally he came to his defining sentence which summarised all his problems: "Whenever I meet a woman, I want to marry, she's always got all this 'stuff' to sort out and 'things' she needs to change!" he snorts. After that he went quiet, looking like he had just justified why he was still single. Which, of course, he had.

Now, how do I respond? We are in the dangerous territory now that the 'stuff' word has just been raised – which implied Simon has issues with the way women live their lives. Now there are a number of different thoughts floating through my mind, from feeling slight relief for the women who have escaped, and marvelling on the fact that this is the first time 'stuff' and 'things' had actually saved anyone from a life of hell. The second thought I had was "You're an oversized male chauvinist pig, why on earth would any women want to go out with you, let alone marry you." To Simon I say, "Trust in the Lord, He knows your heart". With the sort of tone that implies I have nothing else to say, other than words that could really hurt! I sigh inwardly and pray for the right words to tackle this most treacherous of subjects

The trouble is, I really like Simon. In many ways, he is no different than all the rest of us, just a little more extreme. He might be completely useless when it comes to relationships, but he is a good man. In all the years I have known him he hasn't missed a meeting, even if he is too loud and the smell of rabbit-hutches emanates occasionally from his armpits. You also couldn't ask for a more willing helper, from cleaning the church to giving lifts, Simon is pure gold. However, he won't change. He wants others to change around him so that he never has to face up to his now well-established routine of bachelorhood.

Singleness is a major problem for many forty-something people that genuinely feel they are missing out on companionship, children and obviously sex. All the while, life seems to be racing ahead of them, not giving them a chance to catch up and deal with what it is that's keeping them single. The feeling of being a victim to life's unfair throw of the dice is hard to ignore, but feelings about self tell lies more often than telling the truth.

Simon felt that women had 'stuff' which I suppose is something he would have heard them say about themselves, but Simon was really excusing his own bachelor ways.

"Simon?" I enquire with more bravery than before. I know you would think that as a pastor I could say what needed to be said, but experience leaves me with the scars of telling the truth to people asking for help who didn't want to hear it. "Do your mates ever come round to your place to hang out?" I know the answer but need him to fall into the trap I'm trying to set.

"Oh not really", he slowly answers. He knows that he's caught and nonchalantly continues, "I like to get out and about, and you know how it is."

I grunt encouragingly and continue, "Why don't your friends come to yours?"

He squirms in his seat and runs his hands through his balding scalp; the atmosphere becomes torturous as he tries to find words that make him look great. At this point I really do feel sorry for him. I too have been cornered by my pastor and the need to paint oneself in the best light possible is almost too much to bear. We continue speeding past the blur of hedges and trees, the occasional stone croft with broken gate and rusty car fly past as if we were the stationary occupants on a ride at Disney.

"Er, you now how it is, a single bloke's pad is not the place to hang out with mates?"

"Isn't it?" I retort as the car's rear axle inexplicably sends the back of the Capri momentarily heavenwards, sending my voice into realms only women on speed should be able to reach.

Simon laughs until tiny beads of sweat appear all over his purple face, I laugh with him in that casual 'aren't we all having a jolly time' way, but only to disguise my frustration at not getting down to serious issues. I seize the opportunity of his jovial attitude and continue, "Simon, you're a bachelor. That's how you live your life. You scratch your nuts in public and only wash when your cloths refuse to lie down. Your flat smells of a 3 week old lamb kebab and your curtains couldn't be drawn back to see the light even if you wanted them to. You hang out with equally single men all of whom if put together, couldn't come up with a single sentence that would make a woman feel special. You're 44 years of age going on 23 and have forgotten to check the mirror to see what women really see when they are looking in your direction. A 20 something is no more likely to agree to a date than Britney Spears is going to knock on your door and tell you she's been so wrong up to now and it's you she's been looking for!"

The car falls silent as the smile tumbles from his face. I've released a barrage of statements hoping it will shock him into reality. Nothing is left from the previous moment of laughter save the purple face which now hangs with deep disappointment.

"She won't?" he whispers in broken modulation – a twinkle in his eye betrays a face that is trying to look offended.

"No, she flipping won't", I swing a play slap across

his head as he negotiates the roundabouts that surround the city limits. "You don't give up bachelor-hood when you get married you give it up the day you desire to build a life with the opposite sex. There's no 'stuff' or 'things' about it; just simple understanding of how to give and take, more give than take!" I leave the sentence hanging; he seems to have received it well; how well will be proven by time and results. For now I'm happy Simon is happy having heard what he needed to hear.

CHAPTER 5

More things about me

We are all manufacturers. Making good, making trouble, or making excuses – H. V. Adolt

Over the years things have happened to me that still defy explanation, at least from me. Why would I humiliate myself by implying that a reasonable explanation could be found? No, far better to assume the power of 'things' continues to blight my life with the repetitive force of a nagging woman.

Some years ago, before I had formalized my excuses, and simply accepted all events as the normal outcome of a person who is disadvantaged with poverty and incredible stupidity, I found all sorts of events unfolding before me.

Before I became a pastor, my lot in life was to own and run a furniture manufacturing company. We specialized in bespoke furniture, generally made from pine and oak. I was the type of boss who enjoyed taking on all sorts of responsibilities, should the need arise (if a member of staff was not able to turn up for work I'd leap into action and fill their post). Such actions often found me in the finishing shop where all sorts of explosive liquids were available for entertainment purposes. On one such day, when the summers were long and hot and children respected their elders, I was clearing a huge pile of old timber that came from the off-cuts the various projects being undertaken in the workshop at the time had produced. These were then built into an enormous pile for our monthly bonfire. Having our workshops on a farm we could build the biggest bonfire we wanted, which of course we did. On this occasion I also had 20 litres of old cellulose thinners which needed to be sensibly and safely disposed of. Now, to the uneducated, thinners are about the most explosive and dangerous fluid you can get near a flame. So without hesitation I emptied the entire contents of the drum onto the as yet unlit bonfire. Now don't call me stupid just yet, for safety I left a trail to the fire about 15 metres from the huge pile of timber off-cuts.

I was well aware of the danger as only the previous year when my workshops were situated at my parent's house, I nearly blew my mother into glorious paradise. This was when we had found that placing empty thinner drums on an intensely hot fire caused them to explode in a deafening bang. The explosion was caused by the end of the drum being catapulted hundreds of feet (or so it appeared) into the air, a hot spinning disc of shrapnel about 18 inches across would whiz with deadly intent, as it rotated itself back down to the ground, as if looking for some living creature to decapitate. More fun could not be found on a Friday afternoon!

Now, such an act needed a safety station somewhere in the Nevada desert where one could run and hide while waiting for the atomic fall out, not deep in the Sussex countryside. On this particular occasion my brother and I had omitted to mention to mother the exact contents of our little bonfire for obvious reasons. So while hiding a good distance away from the launch site we see our ever-patient mother wandering, clueless toward the fire with a huge pile of boxes she needed to dispose of.

Her happy face and innocent singing is burnt into my mind as she wandered perilously close to certain dismemberment. My mind raced ahead and was filled with horrible images as I instantaneously imagined her in various forms of impalement or horribly burnt. My mind then went one further as I imagine trying to explain to dad that all these body bits I'm sheepishly giving to him used to be mum, and if he sticks them back together with a bit of luck she'll be right as rain! As these horrors race through my mind, my brother has rugby tackled her to the ground just as the first drum went off. After severe threats of a good 'slippering' (the idea of mother taking the slipper to two married men was in our mind, quite ludicrous, but in hers was a very real option) we return to the safety of our house and had a good laugh over a cup of tea.

My cellulose soaked bonfire was built in a field unused by its owners, a good 200 metres from the workshops. Its grass had not been cut for many years, so access to the fire was through a trail made by the constant treading down of long dry grasses, stinging nettles and killer thistles.

As this was one of the hottest days in the year I was

wearing my usual safety clothing as recommended by the Kevin Upton Institute of Health and Safety: denim shorts, nothing else, not even underpants, way too hot for stuff like that! The workshops were hot and sticky with the constant hum of saws, planers, routers and various other bits of machinery. The finishing rooms were even worse, closed off from the outside world, they were free of dust and any other impurities that could ruin the polish of a new dining table. Trouble was they also lacked enough oxygen to keep a small rodent alive. This was why I found myself on many an excursion to the wider and more exciting world of fire building.

Excited by the prospect of making an explosion Al-Qaeda would be proud of, and also very keen to impress the new apprentice (who wisely doubted what I was doing was safe and decided to keep his distance). I took my box of matches and in, what felt like slow motion, struck the match. Now, at this point, the lit match was supposed to be dropped on to the trail of thinners placed on the ground where it would race back to the fire and explode with great force. However, I had not taken into account that thinners behave very much like petrol on a hot day. It expands and evaporates into a dangerous mix of oxygenated fumes. The match never left my hand as the entire field exploded around me in what sounded like the deep woof of an enormous dog. All I can remember seeing is a ball of orange and red flames roll up my body and over my head. It happened so quickly that I was still in my stooped position, as the flames died away, save for a few patches of field and, of course, the bonfire itself. I wasn't sure whether I was burnt alive or miraculously escaped until I saw the motionless face of my apprentice, his jaw hung like it had been dislocated and his arms strung out from the side of his body like he was hanging onto imaginary railings.

"Am I burnt?" I scream, desperate for him to laugh and say no it's fine, but he didn't, he just continued staring with his jaw now so far distended it was resting on his chest. Not wanting to wait for him to come to, I turn to run back to the workshops but find that running now involved the strange motion of keeping my arms and legs completely straight and rocking from side to side like I was in some terrible zombie movie from the 1950's.

I eventually made it back to the workshops whereupon I met the laughter of several brothers who would think it funny even had I just walked in with a severed limb or two thrown over my shoulder. Being the youngest of a very robust family means one has to deal with little sympathy and plenty of mocking. Not that I'm complaining, it provided a very strong family environment to grow up in.

There was now a quick debate over whether my injuries were worth a visit to hospital (we were not hospital type of people, you had to have your brains falling out the side of your head before it was considered a real wound) so I was promptly placed in the delivery van and sent back to my wife instead. By the time they had driven me the 5 miles back home I had also been renamed "woof" as this was the last sound we all heard as the flames licked around me. I rocked into the house through the kitchen door in my now well practiced zombie dance. I was met with the shocked faces of Cheryl and a neighbour who was getting a courtesy hair cut from my brilliant hairdresser wife.

Now I have rarely found a woman who is useless when it comes to family emergencies, it's part of their instinctive abilities, like pigeons who know how to fly home from anywhere in the world.

Cheryl dropped her scissors, rushed me into the bathroom and ran a deep cold bath. The neighbour was left with half a head like Jennifer Aniston and the other like a ragged Afghan hound. Not that I cared, by this time I was going into shock, as my body took over from my mind and decided to do a St Vitus' dance.

As Cheryl ran the cold water into the bath I made the most amazing discovery. "Look I've got legs smoother than a baby's bum." Cheryl's eyes flashed in dismay as she scanned my reddened body from top to toe. Not one hair remained, not even in my nostrils. "Bet you'd kill to get legs as smooth as this?"

She narrowed her eyes and pursed her lips as she guided me gently into the soothing cold water.

"No, seriously", I continued, "with a bit more practice we could get the flash just right and woof it's gone. Every woman in the country could get total hair removal courtesy of my new invention; just need a little less thinners I think ... " I mused further, "We could call it 'Hot Flash' the hair remover that will remove hair quicker than conventional razors with only slightly more grazing ... mmm", I muse, "I think my pain may give me some gain."

Later that evening after Cheryl had settled the children into bed I sat in the lounge gently covered by a towel supping my evening coffee.

"What in the world possessed you to do such a stupid, irresponsible thing?" she queried.

"Oh, you know how it is, things just went wrong. It would have been perfectly safe if it ..." my retort was abruptly interrupted.

"Things didn't go wrong; you went wrong when you decided to set light to 20 litres of thinners".

I knew I was cornered and needed to create some space so as not to get too much blame heaped upon me. After all, I was burnt the entire front side of the body and felt I was due some serious sympathy. The last thing I needed was to take responsibility; all I'd get then was rough harsh treatment.

I went for my lovable rogue look, winked and turned my irresistible smile toward her. Cheryl is a strong no-nonsense type of woman but I can still win her around with my armoury of naughtiness and cheek. Such abilities may have gotten me out of a conversation hotter than my recent burning, but in light of my mistakes and blunders over the years I wonder if I would have been wiser to stop blaming 'stuff' and 'things' and listen to what really was taking place, maybe. Still, after all, the skin grew back and I can look back at a great wheeze ...

CHAPTER 6

The stuff of Devils

Excuses are the nails used to build a house of failure –
Don Wilder

Lucy is 75 years old and she is at that point in life where she can tell you her age in every single conversation and it's the only thing she can consistently remember. She is normally detected by a piercing shriek of laughter followed by an almost supersonic "Hallelujah" which is then of course followed up with "I'm 75, you know!"

Lucy is loved deeply by the congregation; she has a zest for living that is not found in people half her age. She never misses a Sunday morning service or a prayer meeting and enjoys being an active minister in the church. Lucy takes it upon herself to pray for every person in the church. She would pray for leaders and newly saved alike, and never hesitated to bring prophetic words galore, with pictures and scriptures. Everyone felt touched by Lucy's dedication to them. The power of her words was debatable, although she never crossed any serious line. She simply liked to bless.

Lucy is a delight in the church and is a great encouragement to the pastors, but Lucy has a 'devil' as she would put it. Lucy was saved in the Pentecostal tradition and this has affected her thinking and speaking alike. When dealing with a specific trouble, the Pentecostal has learnt to blame the devil, bind the devil, war against the devil, break-dance on the devil's 'tail', spin round and round shrieking in tongues and, if you're Lucy, telling him how old you are, until finally deliverance is found.

Now sadly Lucy has never worked out that such actions are more likely to cause a prolapsed bowel and a sore throat – apart from the fact that the devil has never met Lucy Fraser and is in fact probably deceiving some world leader somewhere in the Middle-East.

Sitting down in her lounge was like going back in time fifty years. Do old people actually never change a single thing in that time, or can you actually buy a wallpaper called 'crazy old lady' and is there a scent called 'musty old man'. She sat on her floral velour sofa with matching head and armrest covers, and poured the tea from a tea set. For Lucy's generation, pastors were special guests treated with only the best china. I find this a little uncomfortable but her fussing is very sweet.

"So how are you doing Lucy?" I ask.

She suddenly loses the sweet smile and sniffs and sighs saying, "It's the stuff of devils" in a deep serious whisper. "I'm an agent of the living God," she continues "and the devil has so many things which he will use to stop me being a minister of life." At this moment she branches off into tongues aggressively beating the devil. (I'm glad I'm not the devil as he's about to get another beating, I chuckle to myself).

"Lucy?" I butt into her savage prayer "Exactly what is the stuff of devils?"

She looks at me obviously appalled that I had not been up all night playing tag with said devils on her behalf. Although she was looking at me like I was the epitome of all things carnal, I was not ignorant of what man makes spiritual and, in this instance, what was making Lucy so distressed. I loved Lucy because she never blamed the pastors or the church for anything. They were always God's chosen, and she always saw them as glorious and triumphant. She would not listen to a negative word being said against anyone. Lucy blamed the devil for every problem she did not understand. When I re-asked the question she began to explain how the devil kept closing her down. As I became more curious as to where she was going with this, I heard a noise as she shifted in her chair that no lady should make. Before I can dare laugh, I cough and to my relief she continues talking.

"When I bring a word to some, the devil will close their hearts and they will turn from the voice of encouragement. They don't understand what they are doing – the devil is closing them down and they are neglecting the word."

Now Lucy did not have a clue how she was being perceived by her many ventures, she just loved people and thought people would just love her in return. Her deep inner desire to be loved and needed was not an emotion she recognised in herself, but it was her deepest motivation and empowering factor that kept her ministering for so long. The devil had nothing to do with the rejection of her words – but simply people not mature enough and with not enough grace for an old lady who wants to breathe in your face, spitting salmon paste all over you, before informing you that she is 75 and has 47 grandchildren. This is not the devil and his 'stuff' – but simply an old lady who knew nothing about people skills and struggled to learn any new teaching on them if they did not include chapter and verse from the Bible.

Lucy needs to be loved, valued and encouraged. She will look for people to do for her what she does for others. Her sense of self-worth is locked up in how others respond to her encouragement. She would have you believe that her self worth and values are fully established in Christ. Although her Godly character is truly shaped by salvation, no person is entirely a spiritual being, so Lucy found the more she brought encouragement the more she was fed with the love and affection her soul craved for. Unfortunately she became so good at getting her needs met she became addicted to giving words of encouragement so as to receive the desires of her soul. Well, easy to say that to you, the reader, but how do you say that to an easily rejected 75 year old who is likely to fart if put under too much pressure! I decided to start with encouragement (always a winner).

"Lucy you're an awesome lady in the church. You have to remember that not everyone is where you are at. I'm not sure it's the devil but simply people's hearts are not able to understand you."

I go on to do ten minutes of training on how to be all things for all men. I'm convinced Lucy will change. Slowly she will give her best and tone down her approach, but Lucy will always need that intense encouragement, so I set some of my key people to just bear her in mind and make sure she gets the emotional foods she needs – after all she is 75!

CHAPTER 7

Paul and Kerry

There aren't nearly enough crutches in the world for all the lame excuses – Marcus Stroup

Paul and Kerry would eat prunes for breakfast and drink fair trade tea, their commitment to live a life according to their convictions was commendable. Their clothes were purchased from the local country store and came in every shade of green you could imagine. I began to believe that their clothes were actually dipped in cow pats to achieve the varying shades of 'cow pat green'. However, considering their intention was to wear carbon free attire, if my cow pat dipping theory is correct it completely defeated the purpose, not to mention the issue of their skin being raw and itchy from all the green scratchy wool – but as a good pastor I didn't tell them. Paul and Kerry met at university and it was love at first sight although I prefer the image of her walking past him and their itchy woolly green jumpers velcroed together! He fell in love with a woman who shared his conviction of not shaving.

As this most well meaning of couples start every day, their troubles go before them, although to me, it will be recounted as 'stuff' and 'things'. I have known Paul and Kerry for almost as long as I have been a pastor and in all those years a recurrent theme would surface in our conversations together. "God has been dealing with a lot of 'things' in my life." Often followed by a commendable, "but I'm overcoming". This was always a relief as they were not inviting me to inquire what the 'things' actually were. Paul never did share with me any issues that affected them, he acknowledged that there were 'things' going on and quickly instructed me that he and God were dealing with them, this gave him the feeling of being open and honest and submitted to the changes God wanted to make in him, without actually dealing with them. Yet, the patterns and cycles in their lives were increasingly obvious.

Paul and Kerry were basically a couple who had an opinion on everything, and were always right! However, unfortunately they couldn't agree with each other on, well ... everything, and all hell broke loose when they didn't. Paul is an avid supporter of the church – he is an avid supporter of all churches which is a little awkward as you're never quite sure who he's off to bless with his presence next! This meant using him in any serving capacity was useless as he would simply not show up. He would get a feeling from God and was gone for a week on a mission to some free Presbyterian church to be a blessing and bring his vision of the gospel to them, usually followed by a very forthright discussion with the minister upon which Paul swiftly moved on.

Kerry on the other hand has a social agenda, second only to Bob Geldof, she would right the wrongs of every victim of society – whether they want it or not! She is an activist without an activity, a warrior without a war, but more frustratingly for her a messenger without a message, not to mention the youngest grumpy old woman you'll ever meet. Her laugh was only ever set free for sarcastic effect.

Paul and Kerry were brilliant at many things, yet rarely did we see any results of their gifting, and as for fruit there was more fruit in a cherry cola than in their lives. Every task got sidetracked by a deeply intense super-spiritual 'leading' that always led to nothing. They were an inseparable duo fighting the world, fighting the church and, as a result, fighting each other!

My emergency call came not from our organic duo but from their ever patient connect group leader who had just suffered one disastrous evening too many. Paul and Kerry had released a barrage of self opinionated statements against the group, the church and ultimately against each other. The evening meeting had finished early as some left crying, others left offended while still others stayed so as to make sure Paul and Kerry left!

"What on earth caused them to do that this time?" I enquired.

"Something to do with the 'stuff' we have going on in the church and how it wasn't why he joined in the first place."

"What does that mean?" I enquire.

He grunts, "Your guess is as good as mine!"

I put the phone down slowly, reflecting with certain doom on the unavoidable conversation that was about to happen. His call triggered in me the fear that had haunted me from the day I met them. It was time to find out what all this 'stuff' and 'things' they are always talking about really were.

My ever sweet wife walks in with fresh coffee and enquires, "Why the long face?"

I take a good long slurp of pure caffeine (a great replacement to anointing when one is feeling carnal) "it's P and K."

In a house of kids we had grown used to talking in code so as not to ignite the attention of our children while talking about people and their problems. However, the kids are now almost adults and any code was broken years ago. Our conversations now are well out of earshot but still the habits remain.

"Aha," she replies. "So you're finally going to find out what all this 'stuff' and 'things' are. It's like some Agatha Christie mystery – when you find out who did it, that's the end."

Well, maybe it should be the end; some people are so full of their 'stuff' and 'things' that just their very presence makes the church shrink! Seeing them walk in on a Sunday is like watching Moses split the Red Sea. Suddenly people would disappear to the left and right. At first I was extremely annoyed with my leaders as I wanted everybody to be loved and cared for regardless of who they are. Eventually, though, I got the distinct impression even Jesus was doing a runner!

I have time and energy for anyone but people who cause the church to shrink. Paul and Kerry fell into this group quite some time ago and, if not for my own procrastination, the good people who call our church home would have been much happier a year or so before!

Why is it that while I'm having to deal with the King and Queen of 'stuff' and 'things' that I have to deal with a 'thing' in my own life that, well quite simply, I don't want to face up to? I am always amazed that when other people puke-up their own stuff I have to dig deeper into me and overcome my own excuses just so that I can navigate myself through theirs.

To procrastinate is to give oneself a well earned rest from the inevitable horror of facing a decision you don't want to make, or so I affirm to myself while once again I find another urgent job that needs sorting.

"The 'things' I need to do are quite extraordinary!" I confess as strongly as possible to my ever patient (heaven knows she needs to be) wife.

"Really, like what?"

Her questioning retort is fired at me with such force I know she isn't even interested in what I have to do, but rather why I am putting it off. I am placating this issue one more time and she knows it. You can't pull the wool over your wife's eyes unless it's from Kashmir and made by Jasper Conran, and this excuse was made more from bull than sheep.

"Well?"

This time her arms are folded and eyebrows rose in that fashion that says, "Give me another one of those crappy answers and I will start lecturing you on hard work and perseverance." At such moments a man is wise to subject himself to his wife. You can't win when you're wrong, and your wife knows it!

"You know how it is; I just don't want to phone them. I feel like Charlie Brown: if I hear 'Lucy' speak any more rubbish to 'Linus' I'll be sick."

"Look Kevin, if you shilly-shally one more time this

church will pay a heavy price for putting up with this garbage."

She grabs my coffee from my hand, sips it gracefully, smiles like the princess she is and wafts out of the room in the knowledge her forthright wisdom had left me with no option.

Flip! She can put me in my place when she wants to! A wry smile creeps across my face as I realise that only a woman can speak in such a manner to a man. If I ever had opportunity to return the wisdom the language would have to be oh so much gentler.

Now, of course, I on the other hand wanted to bury my head still further. I can't really explain why, just some 'things' are too difficult to face.

The fear of a 'thing' is often more powerful than the 'thing' itself. When you face a 'thing' it becomes what it really is and fear disappears. My 'thing' is that I procrastinate over a situation when I have no idea of the outcome or what is going to happen. Your imagination can run away with you so, it's easier to call it a 'thing' and put it to the back of your mind where all the other 'things' collect like unwanted mail that has yet to be filed or binned.

I phoned Paul and found him in his chirpy 'I love the entire world' mood. Great, I think to myself as I arrange a lunchtime appointment with him and Kerry. Lunchtime appointments are the best as they have a very definite time restriction, which is always required in such situations. How does one broach the subject of their volatile behaviour when they seem so completely oblivious to their own wrongs while so utterly convinced of everyone else's? I look forward to my date with as much excitement as a man on death row.

Cheryl jollies back in to collect the dirty coffee cup but her real intentions are to discover the outcome.

"I'm seeing them next Wednesday lunch time."

"See", she says while running her fingers through my hair, "That wasn't so painful, was it, and you'll be happy when you've spoken it through."

"Yeah, I'm happier that you're coming too." I drop the bombshell while exiting for the toilet.

"What?" she yells in my direction, the bark launches itself through walls and corridors so that while seated firmly on the throne I can still hear her as if she were standing right in front of me. "And how do you know whether I have things to do on Wednesday or not, did you check my diary?" This time the voice is deep, authoritative and right outside the door!

Feeling much braver behind a locked door, I continue: "You always have 'things' on, I have just taken your 'thing' and transformed it into a real appointment."

Well, the reply could not be printed but the trouble I was in was a most enjoyable distraction and one that caused a good deal of laughter and teasing.

The Wednesday lunchtime appointment crept up on us like a ninja from a B-grade oriental movie. I wasn't sure how it was going to work out but one thing I have learnt is that when you face the unknown the peace of God is easily drawn upon if you can separate your mind from the anxiety of the heart.

You may be thinking that this is a bit of a molehill manifesting as a mountain, and you wouldn't be half wrong. However, when you deal in the people business, the memory of having your head, as well as part your church, nearly bitten off by a volatile and possibly rabid church member is difficult to ignore.

We sat in a brightly coloured and popular fast food chain closely related to Scotland by virtue of its name (the best way to impress is to take your guests to high quality food outlets). I, on the other hand, wasn't out to impress, but get down to business. The coffee in such outlets is surprisingly good though, which may be why our time together took quite an amazing turn that both shocked and blessed us both.

The conversation with Paul started with the normal route of 'things going on for which it was very difficult to describe, but God was helping him through' to 'there was a lot of stuff going on right now'. Which also appeared to be rather vague, but it left me with the distinct impression that all this 'stuff' was somehow my fault or at least the fault of the wider congregation. The peace of God is a precious gift at such moments, because naturally one would want to scratch out his eyes and feed them to the children on the nearby table eating their meal (well, at least there would be a little more nutrition). However, the more appropriate reaction was to do what my wife was doing. That is, to sit there with the sort of smile on your face that says 'I'm so relaxed and happy with life I just look like this all the time.' We all know that we don't, but somehow by God's grace my smile stayed right where it was meant to be.

"So," Cheryl interjects, "What are you going to do now?"

It wasn't so much a question as a command. Paul and Kerry looked at each other in that way that says we have already prepared our leaving speech.

"We feel that the 'stuff' that's happening in the church (hold me down Jesus, I'm going to kill him) isn't where our heart belongs. We don't know where that home is, but by the loving grace of our Saviour Jesus Christ we will find that new place where we can be free to minister in the freedom of the Spirit without restraint (my knuckles go white and blood pressure swells my head,) so we are going to leave, sadly and not without regret."

A long exhalation of air blows from my lips and blood begins to re-circulate in my hands again as inexplicable joy swathes over me, (they are leaving and I didn't have to ask them. "Jesus, you're the best friend I ever had.")

"Oh that's a shame, never mind. Lunch time over, need to go and get all that 'stuff' sorted", I declare in my matter of fact way as if this is just another average day in Aberdeen. I jump to my feet, grab Cheryl, say our goodbyes and leave before they offer to lay hands and pray for us in loud Scottish tones.

In the car driving home, I wanted to shriek or shout or do something really loud, but somehow there was nothing. We just looked at each other amazed at the level of self deception that had invaded their souls. What actually was their problem? None of us will ever know, except for the fact they couldn't control the people around them with their opinions that they had invented and doctrines that were self created. What the 'stuff' and 'things' were, though, will remain a mystery that will never be solved.

CHAPTER 8

Stuff the Excellence

If you don't want to do something, one excuse is as good as another – Yiddish Proverb

To have excellence in the church is, for modern standards, still a new doctrine. Those who came into the charismatic church movement in the seventies and eighties still have a bit of adjusting to make. For theirs is a free, loving, sandal wearing fellowship of chaos. Services start eventually and ramble on for hours with an inharmonious mix of conflicting words, scriptures and testimonies all led by the Holy Spirit. The service will be concluded by standing in a circle holding hands singing 'Bind us Together Lord'. Afterwards they'll drink 'Mellow birds' coffee in plastic cups and eat quiche for lunch.

You may think I'm being a little harsh, but that's where I came from. I once led worship in my teenage years wearing ripped off jeans with a split so large across the backside you could see my Calvin Kleins!

However, here in early 21st century, the need to modernise is ever more apparent. Long gone are the days of OHPs with hand-written and recently smudged words projected on to a dull wall somewhere between the fire exit and the light switch. The church has gone electronic with a variety of video projectors, computers, DVD players and state of the art sound systems. It is against this backdrop of excellent equipment that I ask my church to have an excellent attitude. It's a heck of a lot cheaper than the electronics and even more effective for building the Kingdom of God.

The difficulty with excellence is that we have to overcome habits and lifestyles that fly in the face of doing things brilliantly well. I have often wondered why church members will treat the place and others with such thoughtlessness and disrespect. I came to the conclusion that it's part of our success, which is also part of the problem. Church has become to many a home from home. When you're at home you are more relaxed and at ease than when you're visiting friends or even relations, but it is this environment that reveals how people live and how they treat their family members. I have never met anyone that wanted a badly-run church that was careless and inconsistent, but I have met many whose lives reflect that very attitude in almost all that they do. With their words they say great things, but with their actions they destroy the power of their confession.

They will often want to change, but never quite make the shift. The reason being the benefits of lifestyle change are not attractive enough to make the shift from the comfort of their present habits to the promise of future benefits. It's just too hard to get the motivation to change because despite the fact that our present habits are causing us strife, we also like and enjoy living this way. It's easy and effortless.

With this in mind, may I introduce William?

The small function room at the top of the church heaved with attendees waiting to start a midweek training program. The weather was insanely warm and the air became heavy with the moisture of 30 worshipping attendees. The room became increasingly sweaty with an aroma (I imagine) to be more akin to a sumo wrestler's loin cloth. As the room became quiet and ready for the teaching to start, a disturbing sound (like that a turbo-charged fly might make) roared and ripped around the room for what seemed like an eternity. Panic broke out as people began to realise the source of this horrific projection. As it was a warm summer evening, there was no extra clothing to pull over mouth and nose. The screams, gasps and clattering of feet were only superseded by the insane chuckling of a man whose whole posture says: "That was me and I'm proud of it". I didn't know whether to run for cover and then thump him to death with a blunt instrument – or the other way around. But what happened next unfolded like a pantomime.

One of my more demonstrative ladies, whose disgust of such activities was extreme and unforgiving, ran to some secret hatch and returned with an air freshener and proceeded to empty the entire can on our human whoopee cushion. Her husband had informed me once that he was required to step outside for such activities for, as she put it, "Popping the cork is an extra-marital action which cannot be performed in the house". The additional stink of air freshener only added to his delight, not only did he drop a stinker capable of disintegrating our nasal hair, he was now the centre of attention and had a crazy woman covering him in 400ml of 'apple and cinnamon' air freshener!

As the fine mist of air freshener covered the smell of putrid, curdled, internal gases, calm also fell and people began returning to their seats – though where William sat there were now only empty chairs. I sighed as I thought what to do? Do I teach on the subject, which, believe it or not, was "How to Maintain an Excellent Church Atmosphere" or do I just ask William to go home until he can be sure that has more control of his "foo-foo" valve.

Church depends upon people being passionate to make it excellent so that the stranger can connect to God in the most excellent way. I am always amazed, though not very surprised by the way people bring the sort of garbage to church that I personally wouldn't want anyone to know about and just simply ruin all the hard work of everyone else.

Lorraine sat three rows from William and was another church attendee in desperate need of training. Hers was a church of self taught faith values gained from endless hours of watching Christian TV and practiced on unsuspecting church members and the general public alike. She knew no boundaries and invaded people's space like an uninvited rash. The first time I met her, she came by self-invitation to my house. I did have a meeting on, but she wasn't invited. I was polite in those days and brought her very caringly into the lounge to sit and wait for the others. As she was about 2 hours early, she decided to wander around the kitchen and check out the cupboards to see if we had any food she might avail herself of. Horrified by her cheek and my relative newness to the ministry, I politely asked her if she would be more comfortable back in the lounge. Foolishly I left her alone one more time as I had a number of papers to finish writing.

Cheryl burst into the dining room moments later with what can best be described as a flushed look of horror. "There's a mad woman wearing a bandana and silver earring in one ear going through my wardrobe. She looks like a pirate hunting for treasure".

I thundered upstairs into our bedroom to see Lorraine rifling the wardrobe pulling out and putting back Cheryl's dresses and skirts, "Err, find what you are looking for, Lorraine?" (Inwardly I'm thinking "get the hell out my house you crazy moo!")

"Oh just looking", she replied as if we were a branch of Oxfam conveniently placed on the first floor of a house she just happened to be visiting.

"Well the meeting will start soon, so if you can pull yourself away?" I sarcastically retort.

She wanders downstairs chewing her gum open-mouthed with that look specially adapted by belligerent teenagers though this woman is more than double that age.

I wonder if I could just push …? No better not, she might survive. I chuckle to myself in as evil a way as possible – without being heard. I enter the room as a number of others had come for some prayer and teaching. The gathering of my congregation members stared in horror as Lorraine walked in the room; they clearly knew her better than me!

The meeting started with some prayer which in our tradition of Pentecostal enthusiasm involves a lot of praying in tongues. It all went well for, goodness, all of 3 minutes when I heard this high pitched almost screaming "Pukka-pukka pukka-pukka pukka-pukka pukka-pukka pukka-pukka pukka-pukka". Lorraine, our local pirate, was doing her best to ensure she destroyed my prayer meeting. I stopped the praying and asked Lorraine "Don't you have anything else you can say in tongues?"

I was convinced that this probably wasn't a spiritual language, but if it were really tongues the heavens would be reverberating with the sound of "Pirate-pirate pirate-pirate". She unconvincingly murmurs that she can pray in different spiritual languages, so I continue on with the meeting whereupon in less than 30 seconds I hear a screaming, "Tikka-tikka-tikka-tikka". I put my face in my hands and sob.

I looked around the room and see the inevitable discomfort this woman was causing the others and knew at that moment I was going to have to save my members from certain "tikka" poisoning sometime soon. A few weeks passed with various crimes of insanity and piracy committed all in the name of Christian TV and deep spiritual leadings. None were serious, though I dreaded a visitor meeting her face to face. Actually I dreaded meeting her face to face but my dread was a definite reality!

Lorraine was easily found in a crowded church after the service. Just follow the freakish laughter and parrot droppings and, sure as Captain Jack Sparrow, she would reappear, causing yet more chaos and embarrassment. On one occasion she was trying to tell a new attendee that she was the church prophet and they should come to her for spiritual knowledge. All the while she pulled gum out of her mouth stretching it down to her hips then proceeded to chew it back into her mouth, not unlike a cow suffering some maddening disease.

I wasn't sure who was mad and who was diseased, her or me for not banning her on the day of her arrival? But after a short conversation with Lorraine about how church should be an excellent experience for all, not just visitors, and that behaving like a diseased cow dressed up as a pirate was probably not a display of excellence, her infamous retort only cemented my belief that she was truly mad, "Oh stuff the excellence, when God turns up anything could happen."

"Yes, but", I wind up for my great delivery, "God hasn't turned up, in fact right at this moment He is probably hyper-ventilating into a brown paper bag while He watches you run amuck around His master plan. Did it never occur to you that God created the world with excellence – in fact everything He has ever done has only ever been excellent? So how come it's your right to be as bad and mad as possible all in the name of the international Christian alliance for mad pirates and freedom in the Spirit?" (No, dear reader, you are right, I didn't actually say the last line, but it ran through my mind like subtitles over a bad movie).

'Stuff' has been the excuse for poorly run church for decades. Actually, 'stuff' has been the excuse that has allowed people like Lorraine to ruin all the good work that everybody else has put so much effort into producing. The crime of the church is not so much doing things badly, as it is allowing people like Lorraine to behave so badly. You wouldn't allow people to come into your home and mess up all that you have spent so many hours fixing. My grace for bad behaviour always runs out at the point I see it affecting the lives of visitors and the newly saved.

Lorraine's days at the church were always numbered, but William started to learn how to live life in a more excellent way and went on to become a much loved member of church life.

CHAPTER 9

Timothy stuffed his back

*Difficulty is the excuse history never accepts –
Edward R. Murrow*

Vapors of human sweat hovered over a bundle of recently removed running clothes. A crumpled, sweaty t-shirt, still hot from its occupant, lay discarded over track suit bottoms, once navy blue but now splattered with dirt and almost black from the moisture of its now vacant owner. A pair of mud soaked black and white Nike running shoes seeming to hum like power lines, lay on their side, apparently unwanted. These clothes that had served their purpose were now rejected and it seemed deliberately placed in the long corridor of the church building on the second floor. Such a sight may be considered quite normal, say, for a gym or a utility room, but just outside my office door in a church?

My horrified stare is equally matched by the face of disdain that is made by our church administrator who is trying to pass by this unwanted gift so as to enter the office. Even though she is a youthful 50-something (notice I tread carefully around such subjects for fear of my life), I was shocked at the height she hovered above the filthy garments! In one leap of faith she launched out — her right leg stretched out like a hurdling champion, her left beautifully kicked up behind. I swear the heat and vapors lifted and catapulted her through the office door.

It is unfortunate she has not done any training for the said sport as then she would have known how to land from such an enormous leap. Her landing was more like one would expect from one of the "weather girls" only this time it wasn't raining men so much as a single hail stone of female angst.

She stumbles, staggers, turns and straightens, looking right at me. Her hair had been unloosed from its allocated position and swung quite dramatically across her face. Quite how lipstick smears at such moments is a mystery but there it was smeared like thinly spread jam across the whole meal face of a very angry woman.

"What?" she screeches, her boney finger waving at me (it must be said that an angry woman with a bony finger is to be feared above all) "Is that pile of demonic sweat doing in the corridor of a church?" Her voice hits its high note with special emphasis on 'church'. Her teeth send a fine mist of disapproving saliva in my direction. Just then the office phone rings and she quickly regains her composure and returns to the duties of administration. Meanwhile I am left to discover the mystery of the sweaty and potentially deadly gym clothes.

I muse as to who owns them, maybe the owner was raptured, and I was left behind and, amusingly, so were all of my staff. I momentarily consider what on earth I could have done that deserved to be left behind, when my thoughts return firmly to terra firma. I wander slightly cautiously down the long, dimly lit corridor, past the various doors that lead to cupboards and rooms, the lift doors and eventually the executive loo and shower room. It has been named as such because it's nicer than the rest of the toilets and therefore to be used by me only.

The tell tale sign of lights coming from under the door and the constant splatter of water tells me we have an unannounced visitor refreshing himself at my expense. "Timothy," I holler, "Is that you?"

There is a pause from the splattering, just the continuous hum of hot water being pumped directly down the drain. "Hey Pastor" comes the reply. It's jolly and bright, but it displays a slight nervousness, tailing off into silence.

I continue with a little more force, "Any reason for your waste clothing being deposited outside my office?"

Tim chuckles, slightly too loud to be spontaneous, "I was wondering if when the towels are cleaned someone might throw my clothes in as well?" He giggles more nervously than before and continues, "Er, I knew it was cleaning day ... " He leaves the conversation unfinished like a half eaten sandwich that's gone dry and is now no longer appetising.

In my mind I'm asking, "How the blazes did you get from my office door to the shower room without any clothes?"

The answer goes unsaid so I try a different approach, "Er, why are you here, Tim?"

"Oh", he pipes up feeling much more confident, "I was out running, came up through the city, it was a bit crowded and I flippin stumbled on the curb down at Bridge Street. I think I stuffed a muscle in my back while trying to straighten up, so I thought it best if I came up here, had a hot shower, then did some stretches." Then without further justification, or any hesitation he asks "You wanna go for a Starbucks when I'm done?"

The thought appealed to me, but I still had some issues outstanding, "Tim, you don't have any clothes, and we are not a laundry service, and what were you thinking running through the town with your dodgy back?"

Tim laughed as loud and as heartily as only he knew how. Still leaving the shower to pump hot water directly into the sewage system he continues his explanation. "I have got a change of clothes in my back pack and I have no answer to the other two questions, it's just one of those things!" He continues to laugh to himself as if his reply is quite sufficient and that this is just another ordinary day in the life of a man who took everything as a positive affirmation of his ability to overcome.

What does one say? Tim is a leader and there doesn't come much better, but his stuffed back is only the symptom of a man who doesn't know how to back away from a challenge. In his mind the things that happen to him are simply the experiences that life throws your way when you are in pursuit of success.

I decide to take him up on the coffee, it's time we had a talk about pace and strategy. Tim, on the other hand, is always willing to go for coffee with me or one of the other pastors as it enables him to spend more time with people in top level leadership. This is why I have time for him, he is a businessman with an eye for good deals, but more than that, he will always tackle his own limitations and work out how to overcome them.

Most people spend their time looking at the external issues in their life that limit them, like how much they earn or why their spouse is crabby in the mornings etc, and so they either complain or give up because they are so difficult to change. Tim realized very early on that the true limitations in our life are within and when you challenge those you find ways of changing your external limitations. My strategy is raising many more 'Tims' in the church, people who have a 'can do' attitude and don't see obstacles as road blocks but simply an opportunity to prove that God is with them; and that when the Bible says we can 'do all things' it wasn't poetic rhetoric, but simple truth set in stone both unshakable and unchangeable.

However, Tim is still naked and in my shower, a thought which sends shivers down my spine. "Tim" I shout again "you ready for Starbucks?"

The door clicks open almost instantly and a tall young man with freshly toweled hair standing at bizarre angles and a smile that spoke of pure cheek lurches toward me as if he were the one who had been doing all the waiting.

"I hope you showered away all that body hair of yours, heaven knows what it'll do to the drains; you know you moult like a hairy dog!" Before I can continue with the insults he is half way back down the corridor and picks up his running clothes that by now have taken on a life form of their own. I stare in amazement, "And what about your back?"

"The shower has loosened it up," he rebuts, "and you don't have time to wait for me to do any stretches."

I shake my head with the smile of irony and I run on to catch him up.

We nestle down comfortably in the old shabby sofas that sit in the window of this rather iconic coffee shop. I often chuckle to myself that they put these sofas in the window to make you think that it is like this all the way to the back, only to discover that when inside with your pricey coffee, all the sofas have been taken by rather scruffy looking students and women who like to drink alone while reading Jane Eyre. Meanwhile, you are left to find a battered set of table and chairs that is uncomfortable at best.

We, however, were lucky this time and found ourselves a spot where one could sit for hours supping on caffeine and the pleasant buzz of other people's lives interacting before us like a cinema screen with added aroma.

"So, Tim, pushing yourself too hard again, are we?"

Strong people need direct questions. If not they will run amuck if you don't confront them directly, though one must add that this is based entirely on relationship and the deep personal trust people develop in you.

"You gotta keep fit to stay on top, it's just one of those things." He leans forward to emphasise his words, then squirms sideways in his chair, his eyes narrowing with the pain just to try and find a more comfortable position with his back.

"Your back isn't stuffed, it's injured and 'one of those things' is an excuse for refusing to change your lifestyle to fit into the position you find yourself in, which, correct me if I'm wrong ... (I'm winding up now into my 'I'm right and you're so wrong' *and my voice is getting uncomfortably loud for a café*) ... is flippin' injured through pushing yourself too hard!"

The coffee shop falls a little too quiet for coincidence at the exact moment I stop talking. Men put their heads down into their morning papers, shuffling them vigorously to fill the silent void and pretend they are not listening, while the women just look sideways in that disapproving manner that women do – like when you have to try to let out a quiet fart in public and it rips too loud!

We look at each other in that embarrassed smirking way that men do when they are not sure what to do next, just like we would have done had we been ten years of age. The moment seemed to last an hour yet would have been no more than a second or two before people returned to their coffee shop religion and we returned to ours.

"Would you like a decaf next time?" Tim enquires. He looks me straight in the eye and I can tell that though he is mocking me he has heard my words. As he wanders back up to the counter for a couple of refills I wonder how much he will pull back from pushing too hard. People like Tim can get addicted to adrenaline and the constant drive of having to be successful. It's potentially as harmful as a person who refuses to work at all, though I doubt Tim would see it that way.

CHAPTER 10

Ukrainian Thing

It is better to offer no excuse than a bad one –
George Washington

I found that despite my strong constitution and healthy country upbringing, I couldn't help but dry retch in my throat as I stepped into yet one more hideously vile Ukrainian toilet.

Ukraine is not a common destination of mine for which I am very relieved. Ukrainian people are as sweet and lovely as you could possibly ask for and, over the last 15 years, the churches have grown exponentially. However, the devil lives in their sewage system. It is possibly the most wicked and obstinate devil I have ever encountered. Its far reaching influence has spread far and wide and has become so common, that even the most forward thinking churches have become so familiar with this anal stink-bomb, that they not only live with it, but invite their soft and vulnerable Western friends to use them as well, as if such a wicked place was perfectly acceptable.

My first visit to Ukraine was in 1997. Communism

was still alive though barely and the KGB still strongly evident in every part of society. The communists had a system of bleeding the people and their land dry of every good thing, while as the Lords of the nation they thanklessly returned to them almost nothing. This left a nation bereft of social services and infrastructure, but worse still it left them empty of expectation. Their ability to think and act beyond their poverty was taken away by the local dictator, so even though the nation was now independent, it was still a slave to the indoctrination of several generations. This made change slow and laborious. I was glad this land was not my calling and responsibility! I returned two more times to this huge country once in 1999 and not again till 2008.

Now it's my 2008 visit that prompts my little rant. As I travel through the city of Kiev I note that while many of the horrid grey crumbling blocks of flats still litter the skyline, many new and beautiful houses with proportions larger and more extravagant than anything in the United States fill the blocks of land that had once stood empty and wasted. The roads don't seem overly improved, save a few more motorways, but the trash cans they called cars that once rumbled and coughed their feeble way round the countryside have mostly been replaced with Mercedes and VW. An unusually high number of new cars have their windows blacked out, as if to suppose great wealth or possible mafia connections? Who knows, but you cannot escape the very obvious fact that Ukraine has a lot more money in circulation.

Now, in my very Western and thoroughly ignorant way, one would not have thought it unreasonable to expect the toilets to make some sort of improvement along the same lines as, say, the motor car? I mean if you can exchange a Lada for a Mercedes, could it not at all be possible to change a crap-filled seat-less bog-hole with a clean white sparkling porcelain toilet that flushes?

The answer to this question clearly is no – otherwise the subject would not find itself in my book of excuses!

The very first Ukrainian toilet I ever walked into I left as urgently as I entered! The church was meeting in a room with an average inside temperature of minus two – as certain ex-KGB officials had ensured we had no heating. The room was warmed up by the enthusiastic and rhythmic worship from a congregation who knew that anything but 100% participation would end in certain frostbite. (I did consider trying this in our church at home but felt there might be less enthusiasm for worship and more desire to leave and go to Starbucks!)

After the morning meeting the need to pee had shifted from a background irritation that niggled my bladder to a full on kidney-cramping scream that shouted to me, "Go and take a whizz before your internal organs explode from urine poisoning and the whole world watches as you pee yourself!" Such a thought had me racing in the direction of the most awful stink where I figured the infamous toilets would be located.

It was here I discovered a long line of brown holes in the floor with apparent foot marks for you to squat on while you precariously hovered over certain death to unload your unwanted factory waste. What amazed me was the obvious lack of accuracy these dear people had in firing off their undesirables. After all, if this is a usual Ukrainian loo, then surely they have had plenty of practice at getting it in the hole?

In my mind, vapors appeared to form a brown, misty strangle-hold around my face and neck. My hand involuntarily covered my mouth as if to take control of the situation before my brain can think, which clearly was going to be difficult considering the mind-altering effect these bog holes where having on me. I stagger backward and, despite the knife stabbing pain in my bladder and kidneys, decide there was no way in hell I was going to expose myself in this demonic lair.

By the time we had returned to the pastor's house where we were staying I was cold and clammy as my body began to go into shock. Arriving at the ground floor flat I thundered through the long dark corridors to claim my place at the now most welcome of toilets. The loo wasn't exactly pleasant as the entire sewage system of a 10 story block flushed through a huge rusty pipe that went right through the middle of the bathroom. I didn't care anymore, I could sit relax and flush, aaah sweet.

On my return to this land of extremes I find that we are now placed in quite a pleasant hotel just a mile or two from the church where we will be holding the conference. Despite being built by the side of a busy motorway it is individualistic and quaint. More like a country resort one might find somewhere in the black forest of Southern Germany. I unpack my bags and wander into the en-suite where everything is gleaming and white. I smile to myself with relaxed satisfaction quite unaware of the dangers waiting for me at the church.

Our national conference kicks off at the newly built

church with a great sense of excitement and anticipation. I am in the company of friends and colleagues from England, Denmark and Bulgaria and find that there is more synergy and unity between us than I have experienced before. The conference enters its second day before I need to use the lavatorial facilities at the church, before this I timed my need to go with my return trips to the hotel.

The building might be new but it is also unfinished. Outside the main auditorium the rooms and corridors still have rough concrete on the floors and walls. Wires lay exposed and hopefully unconnected, the only light was that which filtered through the windows – though due to the dull grayness of the concrete it seemed to get soaked up like water poured out on sand.

It was during the start of the second morning session that I knew a trip to the church loo was unavoidable. I had absolutely no idea where it was, as all my previous wanderings through the labyrinth of unfinished building works I had not seen anything that even resembled a toilet. On this occasion though, I was definitely not going to repeat my experience of nine years previously, I don't think my kidneys could stand up to that kind of abuse anymore! My exploration for the loo takes me outside and up what appears to be a worryingly well worn path away from the church. A long muddy trail leads to the end of the property where four old crumbling shacks that look like they were built by a blind man with no thumbs. They lean against each other in what appears to be a last ditch effort to remain upright. More worrying still is Monica the rottweiler who, for some bizarre and twisted reason known only to Ukrainians, guards these toilets with rabid ferocity. If one were to wander up here in the dark in a desperate bid to relieve oneself you would be sure to lose a lot more than your leg. The outside of these latrines most certainly prepares you for what is inside. A classic toilet, once white but now a horrible yellow, seat-less, unwashed and with no water to flush it, greets my eye. I look in horror. It is the epitome of the old Ukrainian mindset toward things that are not on display.

A Demon of Sewage growls from deep within this evil shack at me. It's toxic sulfurous fumes seep out into the fresh air and hang like a cloud of napalm, daring our conference attendees to enter. Even the locals go through what seems to be something more akin to a kamikaze preflight ritual. Genuine fear and trepidation overwhelms them as they have to negotiate the removing of personal items of clothing without actually touching anything inside. This is where I wished I had paid more attention during the gymnastic lessons at school. Mind you, I have never been quicker at taking a pee in my life!

I stumble out of this prison of pee and try desperately to hide my obvious shock, trying to appear normal and unfazed for all the unfortunates who have yet to discover the horror that awaits them. I walk back down the flattened mud path past Monica, who salivates for a piece of me, and think to myself, "I'm going to have to do this many more times before the week is up!"

My next mission before I leave this land is to find out why toilets figure so low on the Ukrainian horizon. I know certain countries have very different attitudes to such personal activities but what I am experiencing here in a 21st century world goes beyond the pale. Once, while in Iceland, I was staying at a YMCA facility. I entered the toilets early one morning only to discover that everything was wide open. The showers were without walls and sitting right next to them were 3 toilets without any cubicles. In an instant I locked the door behind me and had the entire shower and toilet block to myself! However, despite the Icelanders apparent openness to nudity and bottom wiping, their toilets were spotlessly clean.

This could not be said for my Ukrainian experience. No matter how hard I tried, I couldn't get anyone to give me a reason for why their investment into toilets is so slack. A small perverse amount of cultural logic would have satisfied me – even if it didn't answer the question. I received nothing more than a shrug of the shoulders, a dour look of the face and an occasional comment about "It's a Ukrainian thing". Now, we know exactly what this means, it's something to do with the fact that no one has thought about it and everybody else has refused to take responsibility for it. The net result is another generation of inactivity and mismanagement. Cars will be bought and sold, houses will be built and demolished and generations of Ukrainians will live out their hopes and dreams – but in all that time no one will think of fixing the toilet because "It's just one of those things!"

CHAPTER 11

Coffee and Thought

*The best job goes to the person who can get it done
without passing the buck or coming back with excuses –
Napoleon Hill*

The Mountain of cream on the gingerbread latte slowly melted into the cup, which, incidentally, Starbucks like to call a Venti. I personally would have called it a bucket but I'm not sure it would sell as many coffees.

I was here for a few hours so I needed the largest coffee I could afford. I've taken to sitting in this infamous coffee shop for my thinking time. Sir Edward Heath, a one time British Prime Minister, was known as a thinking man. His habit was to sit in the parliamentary chambers simply to think. It was a habit that was not much admired at the time by either his opponents or even some of his own cabinet. The truth is though, that thinking is the one nutrient missing from our lives.

You could, in fact, liken thinking to vitamin C; a vital part of our diet, without which we would suffer all kinds of ailments. The old navy ships that sailed for months at a time were notorious for scurvy which would cause weakness and pain in the sufferers' joints and potentially could lead to death. All of which was due to the fact that there wasn't any vitamin C in the diet. Thinking is your vitamin C. Unfortunately it is also often missing from our lifestyles, which have become overrun with images from the television and internet. Most media stops you from thinking and simply entertains or informs, but doesn't really get the power of your mind actively in gear.

I used to feel guilty for just sitting down out of everyone's way so that I could think. We live in a world that demands targets and sets goals. Every minute must be justified or accounted for, but all I wanted was to sit quietly and consider deeply everything outworking in my life and the lives of those people I care for around me. It was not until a friend of mine, who pastors a very large church in Sheffield, said one day that the church lacks not money but imagination, that I realised my thinking times were of more value than my office time or any other time that other people demanded from me.

People come and go to church, but at no time will they allow their creative thoughts to expand their possibilities. The result is often a predictable church, unable to think its way out of a wet paper bag. However, a thinking church is creative and cutting edge. It can find the solutions to the constantly changing and problematic society that we live in. A thinking church has the vibrancy of colour set against the monotone monotony of tradition and unchanging habits.

People are screaming inside for change, improvement, excitement, value and purpose, but for a large part, their lives wander past them, one day identical to the last, like driving on an endless straightened highway that always seems to bypass their dreams.

The cream had now all but melted into the half drunk coffee. Cinnamon powder speckled the sides of this cup that was by now rather too cool to be enjoyable. I don't know how long I had sat there. Time was neither my master nor I its slave. People had come, sat, chatted, drunk, laughed and left, but I remained watching and thinking. I marinated in the spices of one's vibrant mind: refreshing my soul, just as prayer refreshes one's spirit.

I was taken back to a moment when I was a young business man. My flair for business was more due to a happy positive personality, than it was to any skill or experience. Happy positivity stood me well for a couple of years until the happy times ended. Well, they didn't so much end as they crashed like some automobile wreck one would see in a Die Hard or Bourne trilogy movie.

It was during the recession of the early 1990's and I had a long, hard lesson on how to do life well in difficult circumstances. My moment came in the autumn of '90. We had suffered under the 80's property boom and crash. All my customers had disappeared as their mortgages sucked up every available penny of spending power. Added to the injury of high interest rates was the even more crippling negative equity that literally made it impossible to move home. As a furniture manufacturer and retailer we lived off the money people spent while moving. A new house needs new furniture and in the good times they spent it in their thousands.

I was sitting in my office – which sounds much grander than it was. In reality it was a dark, cramped space stuck within the rafters of a 19th century stable building. Everything was covered in fine layer of sawdust as no matter how hard we tried to ventilate, all the leftovers of our manufacturing somehow managed to find their way onto my desk, filing cabinet and fax machine (remember those??).

Having done my rounds in the workshops I went to the office to crunch some numbers. I knew we were in trouble but I needed to work out by how much.

What happened next was a moment of real crisis for my life. It was such a shock that I sat crippled by fear for the next 3 hours. I had calculated that we had thirty thousand pounds of outstanding orders but we also had sixty thousand pounds of unpaid bills. Added to that was a slow laborious manufacturing system that despite making beautiful furniture was killing our potential for profit.

I sat shaking in fear, staring over my desk looking forward to the polish and finishing rooms that lay in front and below my office. My mind had given up and I had no idea what to do next.

I had spent the last three years doing the same thing and hoping for a different result, but, surprise, surprise, nothing was changing.

For hours my mind did not think, but was simply overwhelmed by the enormity of my problem. The 'stuff' that was killing me was not actually what I was not doing but what I was not thinking. My mind was full of the 'stuff' of years of struggling with business, growing up in a poor family and generally having no experience of running anything successfully.

The answer to my 'stuff' and 'things' did not just appear like a blaze of light. I didn't feel God's arms around me or His wisdom whispered in my ear. In fact, I would say that I had no specific feeling or sensation of God at all.

The problem with Christians basing everything on feelings is that they feel let down by God when they don't feel Him nearby at specific times. God is truth, unchanging, non-negotiating and consistent. His truth is knowledge, wisdom, revelation and power. You don't have to feel Him for 'it' to be there.

I, of course, didn't feel it and neither did I see it, think it, imagine it or get any kind of concept that could cause 'it' to come. I was, at this moment in time, well and truly 'stuffed'!

I left the office late as usual that day. Even when business was bad we were still busy – which really irritated me. I couldn't work out how we had work, but no money. So, frustrated and emotionally wrung out I dragged my sorry self home. I felt like a bony whippet having had a beating.

The next day I determined to speak to my parents about closing the business. My father was my business partner and we had a close relationship in almost everything we did. Despite my father having a more traditional outlook, he was an adventurer and loved to face challenges head on.

I remembered sitting down round the family dinner table – it was a large refectory table heavily beaten from the years of childish abuse my siblings and I had given it. I sat where I always had as a boy. I knew it was my seat because there on the edge of the table were my teeth marks forever immortalised on the edge of the table. For some now unknown reason back in the mid 70's I had decided to see what it was like to chew the table while I waited for my dinner. It was surprisingly soft and very woody with a slightly waxy flavour!

Now many years later I sat pensively trying to bring up the conversation of closing the family business. My fingers played with the rough chewed edges of the table while I sucked up an excruciatingly hot coffee. This can be done by pursing your lips and sucking hard without actually touching the cup. The vacuum causes the liquid to magically siphon up through the air into your lips. The process also cools the coffee. It is very satisfying if not a little slow and wonder-fully childish.

The conversation never really went to plan. My all-knowing mother would say what they were thinking – she would invariably verbalise for my father, not because she spoke over him but because they lived life like one person.

On this occasion, Mum had the words I needed to hear, "Listen Kevin, we have been through much harder times than this and one thing we are sure of is that God will see us through."

That was it. No more discussion or argument and what could you say? My parents had lived through decades of hardship. It was extraordinary that they had successfully raised six children all of whom had flown the nest and were settled in their own homes. No one could argue with my parents on how to see it through without quitting.

That simple statement of faith which was based on

the word of God and all the experience you needed clicked a switch in my head.

I stopped being overwhelmed by 'stuff' and 'things' and started to pursue a faith encounter that would loose my thinking from the rust like seizure it was held in.

I had begun to realise that the 'stuff' that I was walking in could be understood, contained and controlled. Up till now my life was hugely uncontrollable. More events happened to me than I was able to handle. They had swept me along on the white water of random happenings.

Interestingly, something I discovered at the time was that the only way to control a boat in white water was to paddle faster than the water pushing you. If you overturn or lose your paddles you are at the mercy of the river. Hidden rocks, whirlpools and waterfalls all lay as traps to your life. Fear and resignation take control of our lives as we hurtle headlong down the river of chance.

However, faith doesn't believe in chance but in destiny – and on this day back in 1990 I started to paddle faster than the white water of a national recession and build a life God had ordained for me rather than resigning to the 'stuff' and 'things' that life threw at me.

I was back in charge. Not that my bills got paid or my manufacturing improved, but rather my attitude was first focused on God's possibilities and then my responses to those things which God was offering me.

I started to think. Unhindered by fear, I was paddling faster than fear could flow. The possibility of old enemies returning to our lives was always there. If we stop paddling faster than the river, then the river will carry us again wherever it wants us to go.

One of my first business decisions was to increase our prices rather than discount them. It was a decision greater than fear and led me into my destiny. Everybody was selling with massive discounts thus ensuring a sale, but not a profit, and a business without a profit is a business losing money. It had occurred to me that older people without mortgages buy more expensive furniture and while they were potentially more difficult customers to please, they were also pretty much unaffected by the recession.

My second thought was more the recognition of a good idea my brother had spoken of some months earlier. I rejected his thoughts out of hand because I didn't understand them and because I did not want to look weak or something. Interestingly, it was rethinking his pearls of wisdom that helped me realise we had a bad pricing structure that could ruin the business. The new plans we put forward were the ones which would take us out of recession and help us build on our success.

God had come through for me because of two things I had done:

1. I had faith in Him – more faith than you could imagine.
2. My faith got my mind thinking and I thought my way out of my 'stuff' and 'things'.

It was not the last time I would allow 'stuff' and 'things' to affect my life, but it was certainly the last time I would allow them to control me.

As I close this final chapter of this book I want you to realise this simple easy lesson. 'Stuff' and 'things' are excuses for not believing and not thinking. They are simple unnamed events that happen in our life because we refuse to face them head on and deal with them.

Take time to get a coffee or whatever beverage you enjoy to unwind with and spend not moments, but hours unwinding and marinating in your potential and not your problem.

Here's to 'stuff' and 'things'.